HOPEFUL HAROLD & HIS HAUNTED HOME

RORY REA

Hello,

I'm Harold and prior to the story I'm about to tell you, I did not like to talk about myself or let anyone know about my friends and our haunted home. All that changed when I was forced to step outside my comfort zone to survive.

This is my story and tells the tale of the time when I had to try to save my haunted home, my friends and keep my vamp-pa healthy and DEAD.

So how would I describe myself back then? Well, I suppose you could say that I was a little shy, a little awkward, a little odd and a LOT Vampire-ish!

I hope you're brave enough to continue, but let me warn you that my story is stinky, disgustingly silly, scary and very, very offensive to grown-ups.

Welcome to my haunted home...

CHAPTER 1

MAGIC SPIRIT-OMETRE

- YIPEEEEE!!!
- AWESOME
- HOPEFUL
- UH-OH
- YIKES!

For centuries, humans suspected they weren't alone. Ghosts, witches, monsters, and Boogaboos cleverly hide in plain sight using disguises. Spotting them requires knowing where and at whom to look.

These sneaky beings enter your house silently, they eat your favourite snacks while riding your bikes and playing with your toys. But why do they break in? They seek something else from you, your energy from your laughter and joy. By absorbing these positive emotions, their Magic Spirit grows stronger, allowing them to live in secrecy and enhancing their spookiness.

The more intense the joy they get, the more potent their Magic Spirit becomes. However, negative emotions, like fear have the opposite effect.

To safeguard their lives and the humans they depended on, these creatures had to adopt disguises to blend in and appear in the daytime. Revealing their true identities to humans would evoke fear and anger, weakening their Magic Spirit.

BLOOD DONATION
STOP

Despite successfully capturing positive human emotions and effortlessly blending in with humans for centuries, recently these creatures began to pick up a few lazy habits.

Witches didn't bother waiting until dark before going out on her broomstick, Monsters stopped wearing face paint in public and Frankenstein kept leaving body parts all over the town.

All in all, they risked being exposed. Worse than this, they quickly discovered that you humans would hunt them with pickaxes and big sticks for being a bunch of scary, shocking, treacherous monsters.

Terrified now by the human contact necessary for their own survival, Harold's secluded haunted house offered these creatures safety and eventually they all went into permanent hiding.

Perhaps the most exceptional of all these creatures were the fearsome **Vampires...** Harold's family. Contrary to popular belief, Vampires do not need to drink human blood to remain undead. They drink it because they think it is disgustingly delicious and horridly healthy.

To stay despicably undead Vampires also need Magic Spirit. They are the most human-like monster, which means they can harness enough positive human emotions to provide Magic Spirit for all of the other creatures, as well as themselves. BUT only if their true identities remain hidden!

Harold is the youngest in a long line of Vampires who have owned and lived in their family's haunted home for centuries. After his own parents were wiped out due to a lack of Magic spirit. He was raised by his grandfather Vamp-Pa, and an eclectic mix of creepy housemates...

There was magical **WITCH WENDY** who cast spells and made magic potions to create even more scary monsters. If a person or animal where to drink one of the Witch's potions, they would turn into a **Boogaboo.** At first glance the Boogaboos looked frightening, but they were really cute, fluffy monsters with lots and lots of energy.

They loved to play hide and seek and would jump out and scare one another with a loud BOO!

Rumour had it, that one night while flying her broom over a certain Scottish loch, the Witch spilt some of her potion by mistake and the mysterious Loch Ness monster was now a **big fluffy Nessie** Boogaboo!

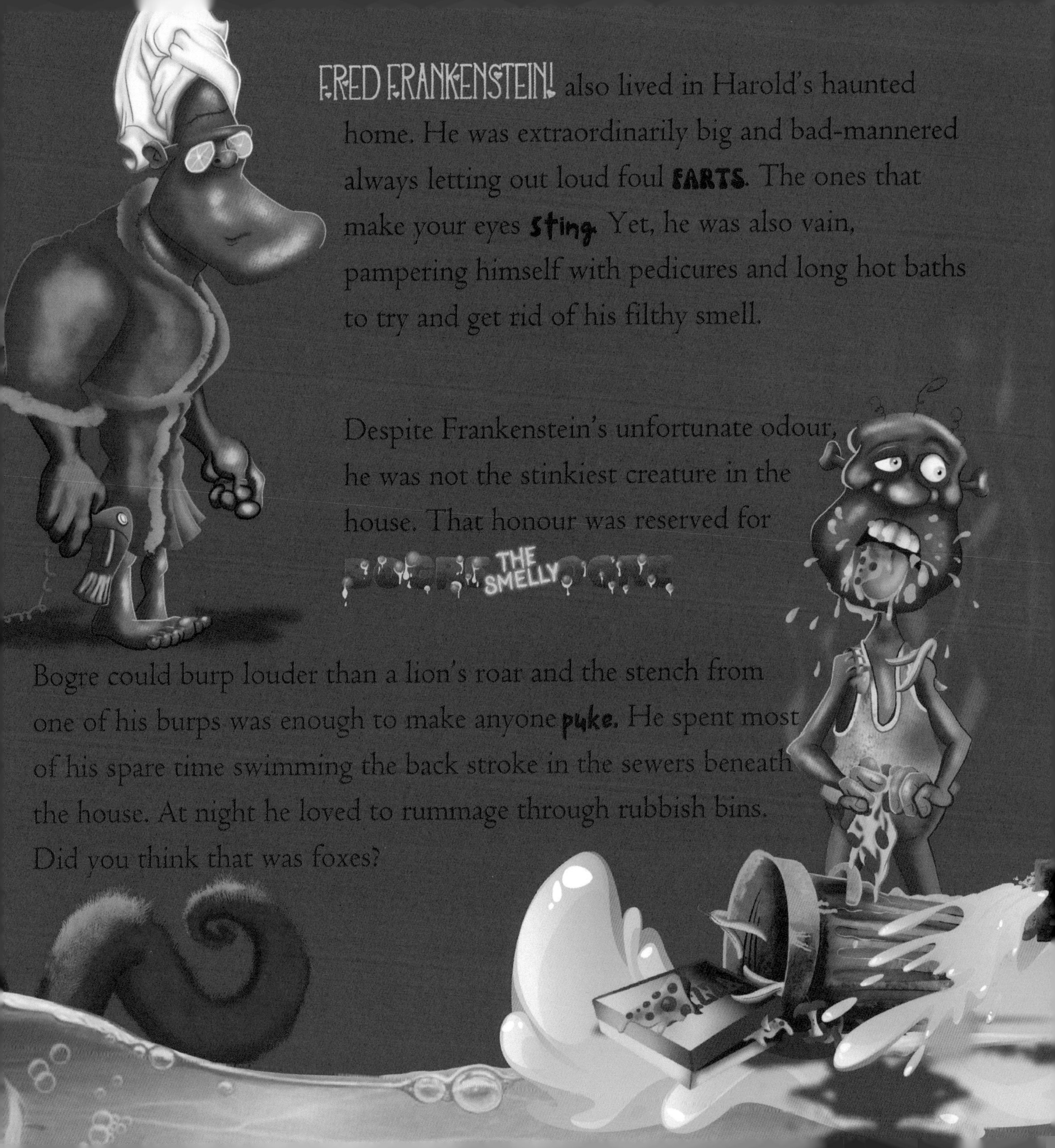

FRED FRANKENSTEIN! also lived in Harold's haunted home. He was extraordinarily big and bad-mannered always letting out loud foul **FARTS**. The ones that make your eyes **sting**. Yet, he was also vain, pampering himself with pedicures and long hot baths to try and get rid of his filthy smell.

Despite Frankenstein's unfortunate odour, he was not the stinkiest creature in the house. That honour was reserved for

BOGRE THE SMELLY OGRE

Bogre could burp louder than a lion's roar and the stench from one of his burps was enough to make anyone **puke.** He spent most of his spare time swimming the back stroke in the sewers beneath the house. At night he loved to rummage through rubbish bins. Did you think that was foxes?

Harold's haunted house was the spookiest of them all, nestled in a forgotten, misty forest, the house remained hidden from most humans. Those who knew of its existence were too terrified to step inside. Whispers of horror surrounded the old, haunted abode, deep within the foggy woods. Some tales were true, while others were mere fabrications. Legends spoke of wailing ghosts serenading the night, or skeletons that jingled, jangled, and screeched. And the most popular rumors revolved around a burping Bogre and a farting Frankenstein!

Driven by fear, the creatures withdrew from public, unable to collect the emotions they needed to sustain their spooky Magic Spirit. Imagining the frightful actions humans might take if they were exposed, they frightened themselves. Would their heads be severed? Would they be imprisoned in monster-proof cages? Perhaps they would even be subjected to anti-monster vaccinations! Their overwhelming fear led to a decline in their Magic Spirit, which they knew would eventually fade away.

The dwindling Magic Spirit had plunged Harold's vamp-pa into a deep slumber, resting in a creaky old coffin hidden in the basement. Harold and his housemates understood that unless they gathered enough human emotions soon, Vamp-Pa would remain trapped in eternal sleep.

Final notice
MAIL

On a bright, sunny day, terrible weather for a vampire, Harold faced another problem. The postman, one of the few who knew about the haunted house, arrived with an unwanted letter. Shaking with fear, the postman cautiously approached, hoping not to disturb the eerie silence. He slid the letter through the creaky letterbox, but before it reached the floor, a loud, smelly belch echoed from inside. Startled, the postman dropped his letters and fled from the haunted house, crying like a scared child.

Harold's horror grew as he read the letter. The bank demanded a colossal debt repayment, which his ancestor had incurred when purchasing the haunted house. They had a mere sixty days to come up with the money, or they would lose their beloved home.

The news deepened their loss of Magic Spirit. Without their home, Harold and his companions would have nowhere to roam or haunt freely. Where would the magical Witch brew her potions? Where would Frankenstein tend to his scaly skin? And how could Bogre, the smelly Ogre, enjoy his rancid swim without the sewers?

Time was ticking, and Harold and his housemates faced a daunting challenge—to save their home and preserve their way of life.

Harold had to find a solution. The answer was human contact, but as much as he had tried in the past, Harold could never seem to get his human disguise right or make a genuine connection with a human being. In short, Harold found getting to know humans really quite difficult.

Despite mingling with happy people, Harold found they were just too joyful; sad people were a little too miserable for him; he didn't get funny people's jokes and odd people thought he was too weird. No matter what Harold tried to do when interacting with humans, he just could not get along with anyone long enough to make that special connection and harness their Magic Spirit.

Harold was now extremely anxious. Losing the house would certainly be the final nail in his vamp-pa's coffin. He was desperate to find a solution. He and his housemates needed to come up with a different plan quickly.

The Boogaboos suggested selling their fur to the penguins, so they would be warm in the Antarctic. Frankenstein proposed bottling and selling his farts on the Internet. Bogre the Ogre suggested he could teach swimming lessons, but then he remembered he was allergic to clean water!

A few days later, Harold found an ad in the newspaper from a movie company. They were looking for a scary set for a new movie. Harold thought this could be their big opportunity to make money. He knew it wouldn't be easy to convince his monster friends to join his plan, but he called the number right away.

Max, the movie director was chubby, charming and cheerful with a big bushy moustache and a bronzed shiny head. He looked in wonder at the long CROOKED, CRACKLY, CURLING branches on the trees outside. The strange, smouldering light that peaked out through the half boarded windows, and the *sweeping, swirling* leaves that seemed to move in time with the howlS from the chimney.

To Harold's surprise, and relief, Max struck a deal to hire the house on the spot. Everyone was happy. Max had found the perfect setting for his movie and Harold would be able to use the rent money to pay the bank on time. It was the perfect outcome. What could possibly go wrong?

Finally, Harold felt hopeful. With so many humans around to make the movie, he knew his housemates would be able to absorb their positive emotions and rebuild their Magic Spirit.

However, they would need to be clever and careful, using all the various hiding spots and secret passages in the house to make sure they were not discovered. They would only be able to come out in disguise when they had an opportunity to acquire some Magic Spirit.

Harold called a house meeting to explain his plan: everyone must stay hidden, while he pretended not to be a Vampire in the presence of the humans. The silly ghosts must not haunt, the magical Witch had better not cast any spells or turn anyone into a Boogaboo, the farting Frankenstein must bath even more often than normal and not give off any foul rotten odours, Bogre the smelly Ogre should take a long holiday in the sewers and the little Boogaboos should only hide and under no circumstances seek!

Harold knew that ensuring his monster friends stayed hidden would be no easy task, after all they were an unpredictable, curious and mischievous bunch.

It is time to hide and stay out of sight.
The Boogaboos must not be tempted,
to come out and give a **FRIGHT!**

Up in the attic or behind the bookcase.
They all try their best, to find the
perfect hiding place.

Oh, but those silly Boogaboos had too much inquisitiveness and not enough will. For they were not able to keep themselves hidden or sit still.

They couldn't help their curiosity, so came out to snoop, they falsely thought they were a careful and quiet group.

CHAPTER 2

MAGIC
SPIRIT-OMETRE

-YIPEEEEE!!!

- AWESOME

- HOPEFUL

- UH-OH

- YIKES!

As everyone got ready on the set, they heard that a famous actress named Julia would be the main star. Julia lived an exciting and glamorous life, but she often felt lonely. She didn't have a place to call home and didn't have many close friends outside of the movie's.

When she arrived on set, Julia immediately felt uneasy. She put the **errie, mysterious and spooky** atmosphere down to more than just the special effects but couldn't quite put her finger on what was making her so uneasy. Deep down inside, Julia knew not all was at it seemed, Could this house really be haunted? She thought.

Julia was soon distracted from her concerns when Max introduced her to Harold. Julia instantly captivated Harold, his green ghoulish eyes went hazy and his face became even paler than normal . He was lightheaded, a bit dizzy and he thought to himself, I must not have drank enough blood today.

Pulling himself together, Harold closed his gaping mouth, tucking his sharp, shiny fangs back under his upper lip. He had to make sure he didn't let his guard down. After all, he had an important role and needed to fool the cast into thinking he was just an average everyday human.

Julia shared her worries with her co-star Sid, a bossy and brash movie star with an ego to match. Sid arrogantly and airily informed her that he had acted in hundreds of scarier movies and had been on stranger and eerier sets than this one. He sarcastically sneered at Julia's worries, "There's no such thing as scary ghosts, or menacing monsters, or even spooky Vampires!"

Meanwhile Harold's housemates, particularly the Boogaboos, were secretly studying their new house guests. They found the humans attempts at portraying scary characters very funny and began to feel unusually relaxed in the presence of them. For once they didn't have to put on disguises to blend in, as the actors were portraying them instead. Before too long it was difficult to tell where the costumes started and where the real Boogaboos ended.

CHAPTER 3

MAGIC
SPIRIT-OMETRE

- YIPEEEEE!!!
- AWESOME
- HOPEFUL
- UH-OH
- YIKES!

One day, in a break between filming, Julia spotted Harold trying to hide something behind a large, old, dusty grandfather clock in the dark hallway of the house. Given her suspicions, she decided she was going to get to the bottom of what was going on in this strange, creepy house. After spotting her approaching, Harold panicked and appeared to be trying to hush and hide someone, or something, without Julia seeing.

Julia approached Harold, who remained silent, making her think she'd imagined the situation. Just as Julia began to doubt what she had seen there was a teeny, tiny, high-pitched noise,

"ACHOO!"

Julia hadn't sneezed. Harold hadn't sneezed. Could it have been a spring in the old grandfather clock coming loose? She slowly looked down to investigate, only to discover a little, round purple fur ball with big eyes peeking out from behind the old grandfather clock. After pausing in disbelief, she loudly screamed, before running away from Harold and his frightening fuzzy accomplice.

Julia ran fast up the creaky, crooked stairs and down the long and narrow dark hallway, desperately dodging holes in the fragile floorboards. She swore the cold, deathly breath of ghosts where following her footsteps. Flinging herself into the nearest room, she hid beneath a damp, dusty blanket.

The room felt ice cold and Julia was sure she could hear the mould and damp dripping slimily and slowly down the walls. She tried to control her quivers to avoid giving away her hiding place to Harold and his monster pet. Julia thought the Boogaboo was probably going to eat her … one tiny mouthful at a time.

Harold raced after Julia two creaky stairs at a time. He sensed her hiding place and knocked nervously on the door of the nearest room. At this point he reluctantly realised he had no choice and would have to tell Julia that her suspicions were correct, this was not just a movie set and his home was not an ordinary house with ordinary occupants.

Harold explained that his haunted house full of ghosts, witches and monsters wasn't a danger to Julia. He told her about his vamp-pa, how he missed him deeply and pleaded with her to keep his secret so he could save his family, his friends and his home.

Despite feeling shocked and scared, Julia found herself feeling sorry for Harold, after all if anyone could understand how it felt to be alone it was her. Tense, cautious, and very hesitant, she agreed to keep his secret and help Harold.

Feeling relieved and a little excited at the prospect of a human friend, Harold introduced Julia to the Boogaboo. Julia jumped at the sight of the little creature again and nervously asked, "What kind of monster is it?" "It's a Boogaboo and he's very friendly." Harold responded.

Julia looked closer at the Boogaboo and could see the warm, hopeful expression on its face. She realised she had no need to be afraid. To her surprise, the Boogaboo spoke to her in a squeaky voice, joyfully declaring...

"Now say hello to everyone else!"

As Harold struck a match, the room lit up to reveal all the different types of creatures and monsters gathering closer from out of the dark.

The magical Witch flew her broom across the room, a Bugaboo slipped out from inside a shoe and there was another one hiding in the closet too.

Another peeked out from the bedside table drawer, so you could just see its head, then Bogre the Orge crawled out from under the bed.

As the weeks went by, Julia spent a lot more time with Harold and his housemates. She started to enjoy staying in the haunted home. The long, dark hallways didn't seem so ghostly and the floorboards didn't seem so unnervingly creaky. She thought the dirty cobwebs and dusty furniture added charming character to the house and found the howls in the night relaxing.

Julia spent her breaks from filming picking flowers with the Boogaboo's, going on broom rides with the magical Witch and having picnics in the sun with Harold – in suitability vampire shaded spots of course.

Harold also enjoyed spending time with Julia. She made him feel cheerful and hopeful. His worries didn't seem so bad when Julia was with him. Even the Boogaboos liked Julia, they made her an honorary Boogaboo and told her she would always be welcome in their happy, haunted home.

CHAPTER 4

All was going to plan until one particularly long, dreary day of filming when Sid was behaving like an even bigger, boastful diva than usual.

After demanding a break, he heard a bath running upstairs. Assuming it had been drawn to help him relax, he grabbed his towel and rubber duck before making his way upstairs to the bathroom.

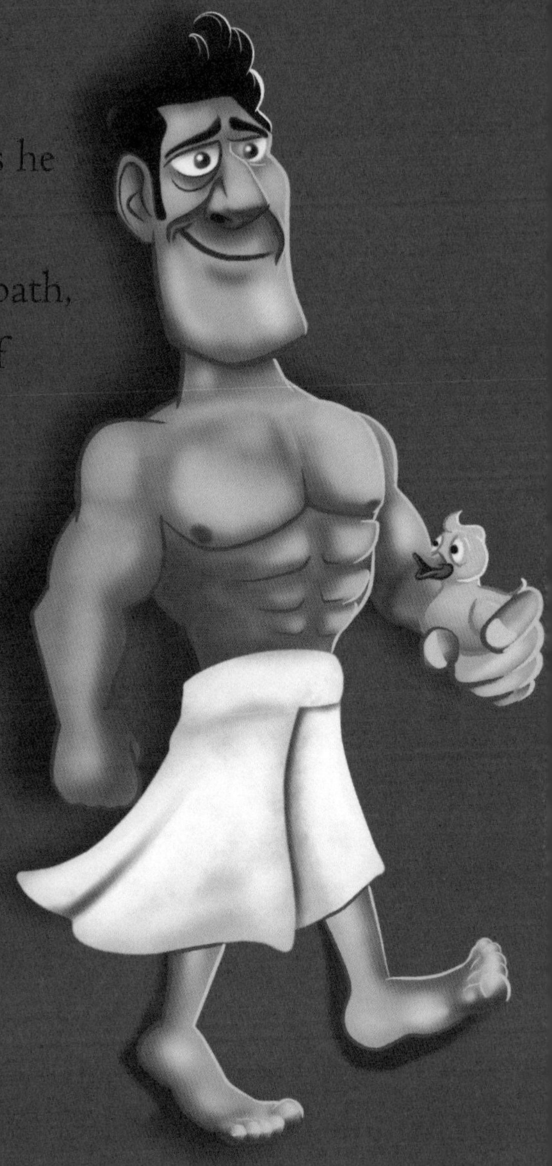

Thick steam from the hot bath hit Sid's face as soon as he opened the door. It was so difficult to see through the thickness of the air that Sid had to feel his way to the bath, before hopping into the tub quickly and letting himself sink down into the bubbles, slowly closing his eyes.

With a relaxing sigh he stretched out his legs, pointing out his tippy toes to the end of the tub.

He stopped abruptly, something didn't feel right. The bottom of the bath felt rough, tough and scaly against his toes. He prodded his feet around and was met with a loud, disgruntled, ghastly moan.

Sid squinted his eyes through the bubbles, peering towards the other end of the steamy tub. A large green blob came hazily into focus. He lent forward and rubbed his eyes ... FRED FRANKENSTEIN!

Leaping out of the bath in a frenzied panic, Sid grabbed his towel and ran in terror down the haunted hallway to get out of the house as fast as he could. He rushed down the creaky stairs shouting, "I QUIT, I QUIT!" and flew out the door in a flash.

Sid ran far from the haunted house, deeper and deeper into the forest, only stopping to catch his breath. Soon he was lost but suddenly a jar of purple soda fell from the sky and bumped him on the head. Before he even considered where it came from, Sid picked up the bottle, popped the cork and in one slurp drank the purple, tasty liquid and let out a relieved, "Ahhh."

Suddenly he felt itchy all over. His hands felt furry, his belly began to rumble and his bare bottom sprouted purple fluff! Just as he was wondering what was in this strange soda – POOF! - Sid transformed into a . . . BooJaboo!

CHAPTER 5

After seeing Sid flee, Harold gloomily realised that no main actor meant no final scene and no final scene meant no movie, and no movie meant no money to save his haunted home! Not only this, but Sid would surely tell everyone about the shocking story of sitting in a bath with a real-life Frankenstein.

Harold's hopes of saving his haunted home had fled with Sid. The crew began to pack up their lights, cameras and equipment as Julia tried to comfort Harold.

Meanwhile, in the bottomless basement – a particularly damp, dark, and exceptionally eerie room of the haunted home where no one had been for a very, very long time – the ancient concrete on the walls suddenly started crumbling. There was the creaking sound of an old, wooden lid lifting off its rusty hinges. Dust flew in every direction and sleepy spiders leapt from their weary webs as a dark, towering figure arose from his ancient, rotting coffin.

Harold and Julia heard distant thunderous footsteps slowly getting closer, louder and clearer. At the same time, the Boogaboo's also noticed that they started to feel a little odd. Bogre the smelly Ogre was feeling tingly all over and looked to Fred Frankenstein only to find that he had disappeared.

Looking up he discovered Frankenstein was floating around the ceiling, along with the magical Witch and the other monsters. Before he could question what was happening, his toes felt light and he lifted from the floor.

Harold and Julia looked up in shock and confusion at sight of the creatures swirling in the air above their heads. Magic purple dust surrounded them and glancing over to the doorway, Harold noticed a dark figure and instantly recognised who it was, "Vamp-pa!"

Stunned, Harold asked how Vamp-Pa was awake and standing before him after all this time. His Vamp-pa explained that Harold had succeeded in absorbing the most powerful emotion. One strong enough to do extraordinary magic and awaken even the sleepiest of Vampires.

Harold had formed a true friendship with Julia, he had finally formed a meaningful human connection.

CHAPTER 6

In the midst of all the commotion, no one noticed another figure watching from the front door of the house. Max, the movie director. Shock had frozen Max like a statue as he looked at the room full of Boogaboos, monsters and creatures. They stared back at him, fearful and not knowing what he would do next. They had been found out!

Max took a deep breath and paused for a second before shouting, "CUT!" Max jumped around, punching the air in excitement, and exclaimed, "What an ending. What great acting. What amazing costumes and special effects!"

He pushed his big bushy moustache right into Vamp-pa's face, tugging on his fangs and pinching his ashen cheeks, "I've never seen costumes or face paint quite as realistic as this!"

In a state of celebration, he hugged and kissed the Boogaboos and thanked them for making his movie spectacular, "It's a masterpiece!" he cried.

Collecting the cameras, he rushed off to begin editing and finalising his movie.

Harold soon received a hefty payment and after repaying the loan, he used the remainder of the money to arrange a special premiere of the movie in his house for his whole haunted family to enjoy. No humans were invited … except for one special honorary Boogaboo of course.

Despite remaining hopeful, Harold had moments where he doubted if he could save his home and get enough magical spirit to also save his friends and Vamp-Pa. he couldn't have wished for anything more than for them all to live together in their haunted home, never mind meeting a best human friend in Julia!

Now that Julia was part of their family, Harold, Vamp-Pa, the Boogaboos and all the other house creatures were able to restore their magical spirit from her positive emotions. They were free to haunt, roam and play in disguise, meaning they could continue to live in Harold's home hauntedly ever after.

THE END

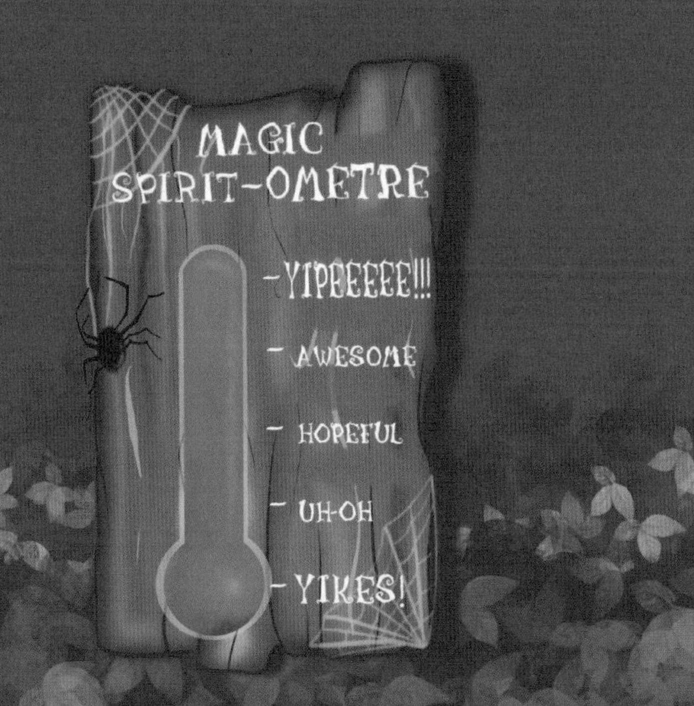

Hey there, brave readers!
Thank you for exploring the spine-tingling thrilling adventure of Harold's haunted house, I would love to hear what you think!

Your reviews are like magic spirit that help me create more exciting stories just for you. So, scan the QR code, and share your thoughts with me.

EMBARK ON A THRILLING
INTERGALACTIC
TALE WERE BRAVERY, FRIENDSHIP AND
THE WONDERS OF THE UNIVERSE
COLLIDE
IN AN UNFORGETTABLE
INTERSTELLAR ADVENTURE

Printed in Great Britain
by Amazon